A KISS FOR LITTLE BEAR

by ELSE HOLMELUND MINARIK

Pictures by MAURICE SENDAK

First published in Great Britain 1969
by World's Work Ltd
Reissued 1992 by William Heinemann Ltd
Published 1993 by Mammoth
an imprint of Reed International Books Ltd
Michelin House, 81 Fulham Road, London SW3 6RB
Reprinted 1995, 1998

Text copyright © 1968 by Else Holmelund Minarik
Illustrations copyright © 1968 by Maurice Sendak

'I Can Read' is a registered
trademark in the USA of Harper Collins

ISBN 0 7497 1257 0

A CIP catalogue record for this title
is available from the British Library

Printed in Hong Kong by Wing King Tong Co. Ltd.

A Kiss for Little Bear

"This picture makes me happy,"
said Little Bear.

"Hello, Hen.

This picture is for Grandmother.

Will you take it to her, Hen?"

"Yes, I will," said Hen.

Grandmother was happy.

"This kiss is for Little Bear," she said.

"Will you take it to him, Hen?"

"I will be glad to," said Hen.

Then Hen saw some friends.

She stopped to chat.

"Hello, Frog.

I have a kiss for Little Bear.

It is from his grandmother.

Will you take it to him, Frog?"

"OK," said Frog.

But Frog saw a pond.

He stopped to swim.

"Hey, Cat.

I have a kiss for Little Bear.

It is from his grandmother.

Take it to him, will you?

Cat—hey!

Here I am, in the pond.

Come and get the kiss."

"Oogh!" said Cat.

But he came and got the kiss.

Cat saw a nice spot to sleep.

"Little Skunk,

I have a kiss for Little Bear.

It is from his grandmother.

Take it to him like a good little skunk."

Little Skunk was glad to do that.

But then he saw another little skunk.

She was very pretty.

He gave the kiss to her.

And she gave it back.

And he gave it back.

And then Hen came along.

"Too much kissing," she said.

"But this is Little Bear's kiss,

from his grandmother,"

said Little Skunk.

"Indeed!" said Hen.

"Who has it now?"

Little Skunk had it.

Hen got it back.

She ran to Little Bear,

and she gave him the kiss.

"It is from your grandmother,"

she said.

"It is for the picture you sent her."

"Take one back to her,"

said Little Bear.

"No," said Hen.

"It gets all mixed up!"

The skunks decided to get married.

They had a lovely wedding.

Everyone came.

And Little Bear was best man.